AF266104

د شمیره کیسه

THE NUMBER STORY

SMALL BOOK ONE

ENGLISH - PASHTO

*Numbers Teach Children
Their Number Names*

written and illustrated by

MISS ANNA

Early Reader Edition of *The Number Story 1*
Bronze Medal Winner, 2016 Wishing Shelf Book Award

Copyright © 2018 by Jieeun Woo
Illustrations © Jieeun Woo

Cover by | Lumpy Publishing
Layout by | Lumpy Publishing
Translated by Ibrahim Hamza
Coloring by Jieeun Woo and Maria Mirabella

All rights reserved. No part of this book may be reproduced or transmitted in any form or by any means whatsoever, including photocopying, recording or by any information storage and retrieval system, without written permission from the publisher and/or author: missanna@missannabooks.com.

Library of Congress Control Number: 2018902040

Names: Miss Anna, author.
Title: Number story : numbers teach children their number names / Miss Anna.
Description: Portland, OR: Lumpy Publishing, 2018.
Identifiers: ISBN 978-0-9962164-5-6 | LCCN 2018902040
Summary: The pictures and rhymes present stories which introduce numbers 0-10.
Subjects: LCSH Numeration—English--Pashto--Pictorial works--Juvenile literature. | BISAC JUVENILE NONFICTION /
Languages: English--Pashto
Classification: LCC QA141.3 .M57 2018 | DDC 513—dc23

Publisher: Lumpy Publishing
Website: www.missannabooks.com
Email: missanna@missannabooks.com

Paperback: ISBN 978-0-9962164-5-6
Printed in the U.S.A.   1 3 5 7 9 10 8 6 4 2

ایا غواړئ د شمېرو نومونه زده کړئ؟

It is very easy and a lot of fun!

ډېره اسانه او په زړه پورې ده!

Say-along our little jingle

له موږ سره زموږ کوچنۍ کیسه زمزمه کړئ!

starting from Number One!

راځئ چی له یو شمیرې څخه یي پیل کړو!

1

یو   ۱

یو زما د ګوتی په څیر مستقیم دی.

ONE!
يو!

2

TWO   trails a tail.

۲ دوه

دوه یوه لکۍ لري.

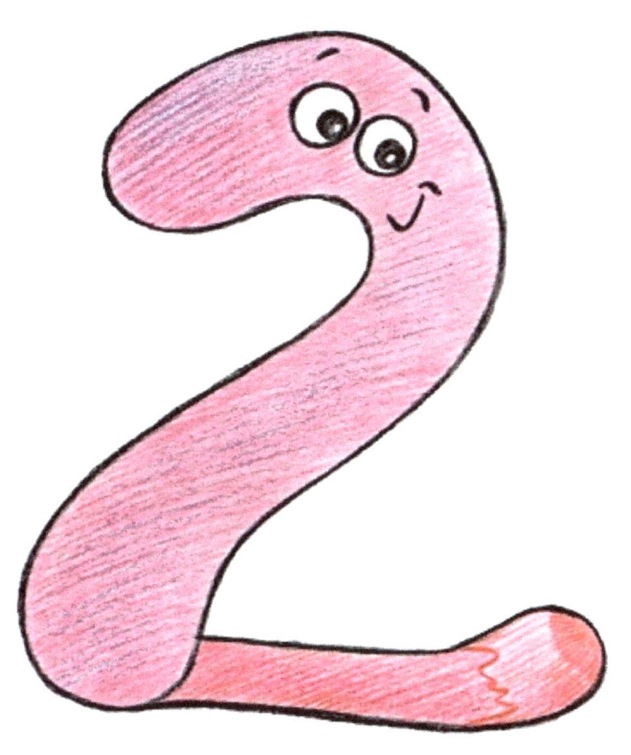

A TAIL! یوه لکۍ!

3

THREE   has bumps.

۳   درې

درې یوې غوندی په څېر ده.

BUMPY!

شنو غوندیو ته وګورئ!

4

FOUR carries a sail.

۴ څلور

څلور یوه بیړۍ ده.

بوه بادوان لرونکۍ بېړۍ!

5

FIVE   is a racing track.

۵ ٪ پنځه

پنځه دسیالی یو سړک دی.

VROOM
وروووم!

6

SIX   curves like a snail.

٦   شپږ

شپږ د حلزون په څېر تاو شوی.

A SNAIL!   يو حلزون!

7

BE CAREFUL! IT'S SHARP!

احتیاط وکړه! تیره ده!

IEIGHT   is rollercoaster rails.

اته ۸

اته یو هوایي اوسپنیز ګاډی دی.

ايپيي!
YIPPEE!

9

NINE is a bubble on a stick.

نه ۹

نهه په لرگی یوه پوکانه ده.

A BUBBLE! یوه پوکانه !

T E N   is an eye of a whale.

لس د نهنګ يوه سترګه ده.

HELLO!

سلام !

And **O**

او

ZERO   is an empty pail.

صفر

صفر يو تش سطل دى.

IT'S
EMPTY!
دا تش دی!

Thank you for playing with us today.

We had a lot of fun too!

نن له موږ سره لوبي کولو څخه مننه.
موږ هم ډير ښه وخت درلود!

We are your Number friends,
Zero to Ten,
Who will be here for you~

موږ ستاسپی ملګري يو
صفر څخه تر لس.
موږ به تل ستاسپی لپاره دلته يو.

Bye-bye now!
See you again soon.

اوس لپاره خدای په امان!
ډېر ژر به بيا سره وګورو!

The Numbers are *SINGING* too!

To sing-a-long, look for Miss Anna Number Story
at your favorite music store like iTUNES.

MP3

Numbers 0-10
IDENTIFYING
& COUNTING

Numbers 11-20
& Ordinals

first, second, third...

Numbers 0-100
& Place Values

ones, tens, hundreds...

About Clock
& Telling Time

hours, minutes, seco...

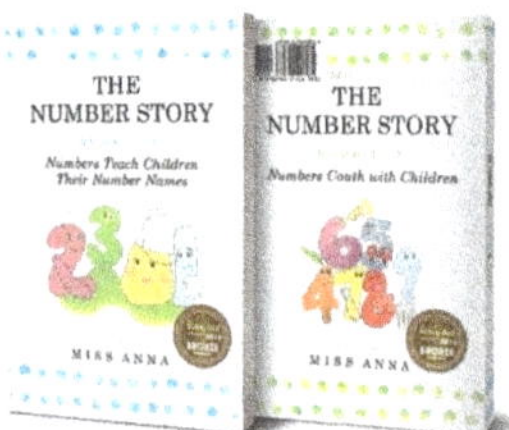

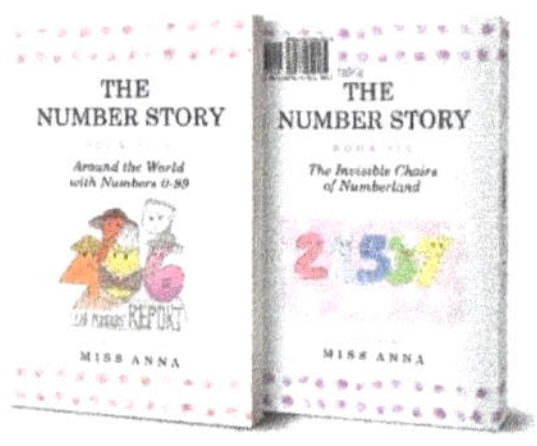

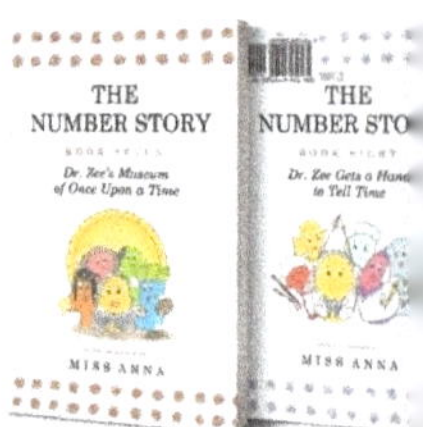

Number Story 1 & 2

isbn: 978-0-996216-48-7

Number Story 3 & 4

isbn: 978-1-945977-01-5

Number Story 5 & 6

isbn: 978-1-945977-06-0

Number Story 7 &

isbn: 978-1-949320-4

For more Miss Anna books to love,
visit us at

www.missannabooks.com

Numbers are working hard all over the world!
Come Travel the World with Us!

www.ingramcontent.com/pod-product-compliance
Lightning Source LLC
Chambersburg PA
CBHW041057050726
47599CB00018B/2188